Clint Faraday Mysteries
#12
Dead Certain

New residents on Isla Bastimentos. They were people no one liked. They were arrogant and vulgar. Bob said they were headed for trouble. That was for dead certain. He didn't mean it quite like that.

Clint Faraday Mysteries
#12
Dead Certain

Contents

About the author

CD was born in Lakeland, Florida. His education is in genetics and botany. He has traveled over much of the world, particularly when he was in music as a rock rhythm guitarist with some well-known bands in the late sixties and early seventies. He has worked as a high steel worker and as a longshoreman, clerk, orchidist, bar owner, salvage yard manager and landscaper – among other things.

CD began writing fiction in 1984 and has more than 115 books published as of this time in SciFi, murder, orchid culture and various other fields.

He now resides in Bocas del Toro and David, Panamá, where he continues research into epiphytic plants. He loves the culture of the indigenous people and counts a majority of his closer friends among that group. Several have "adopted" him as their father. He funds those he can afford through the universities where they have all excelled. "The Indios are very intelligent people, they are simply too poor (in material things and money. Culturally, they are very wealthy) to pursue higher education."

CD loves Panamá and the people. He plans to spend the rest of his life in the paradise that is Panamá.

- Estrelita Suarez V.

CD is involved in research of natural cancer cure at this time. It has proven effective in all cases, so far. It is based on a plant that has been in use for thousands of years, is safe, available, and cheap. He has studied botany, and was cured of a serious lymphoma with use of the plant, *Ambrosia peruviana*.

Information about this cure is free on the FaceBook page, Ambrosia peruviana for cancer. CD asks only that all who try it please report on its effectiveness on that group.

Dead Certain

Lazy Day

Clint was just lazing around the house. It was a truly beautiful day, but he didn't really want to get involved in anything for awhile. His last case had him running all over the country, never quite knowing exactly what was happening until it was almost over. He decided to go into town to chat with people in all the regular spots. He didn't want to become involved in things, but that didn't mean he wanted to be ignorant about local happenings.

It wouldn't rain until mid-afternoon, probably. It was that time of year when it rained for an hour or two in the afternoon, then cleared by nightfall. He would be back before that. If not, he would stay someplace with the chatter until it was over.

He greeted a number of people on the walk into town. Quite a few greeted him. He stopped to chat with several people, then continued. It took him until a little after ten to reach the parque. The regulars were sitting at their usual table at the Golden Grill. They called him over. He sat to have coffee and empanadas and to chat. The talk was mostly about how much rain there was lately and how the old-timers remembered the year when it rained for seventeen days and nights, straight. The way Martinelli should concentrate a lot more on stopping the petty thieves who were stealing the tourists' cameras and cel phones. The way something would have to be done about the boats at night with no running lights. How rude the taxi drivers were in the town. Whatever came up.

There were some people who bought a place on Isla

Bastimentos, in the wrong place for white gringos, particularly ones with arrogant, superior attitudes.

"The Dickerson people? They aren't really so bad," Bob suggested. "They just are used to treating natives like servants. They lived in India for two years, then in the Philippines for two, then the states, now here. I talked with them. They weren't happy anyplace they've been, for long. They always had plenty of servants. They can afford them. They just let it run over into the way they treat everybody they come across. The Indios don't let it bother them, the blacks get all het up."

"Yeah," Aaron added. "They picked the wrong place for their type to try to build anything. Those people won't put up with that crap. Remember what happened to those Fordyce people. They headed back to England with their tails between their legs in less than a month!"

"They chose the wrong place to build. There's gonna be trouble with the locals out there, for dead certain, I'm afraid," Bob agreed.

"You can't tell them anything. They know everything about everything," Tom put in. "I tried to explain, from my own experiences with the people here, that they'll never be accepted. That's true, even here in Bocas. It's true, in spades, on the other islands.

"Well, they won't listen to me, it's their own problem to live with."

Clint had to bite back a remark. He didn't like Tom, at all. The asshole was worse than the people he was supposedly giving the benefit of his great experience. If there was anyone in Bocas Town who knew everything there was to know about everything, who wouldn't listen to a word from anyone who disagreed with him, it was Tom. All the people at that table were accepted and liked by the locals, except him. He was blind to that. He believed everyone native to Panamá hated all gringos. He didn't like Clint, to the point he was rude, because the Indios were such good friends to him. He told everyone new that they had to be careful around the Indios. They would steal everything they had the minute their back was turned. The blacks were thieves to the same extent, and dangerous, as well. The Indios were, at least, mild-mannered and respectful – to your face.

Clint would like to smack him in the puss when he started that stupid rant. He simply was unable to recognize the fact that he was the misfit.

Clint said he'd better get back home before the rain started. Everyone said their good lucks to him – except Tom, who sat there and looked over the parque. Clint made it a point to wish each of them well by name. He acted, as almost always, like Tom wasn't there.

Next stop was home. What to do now?

He read a book Judi Lum, his attractive nextdoor neighbor, left for him. It was written by Dave, his nutty musician – botanist friend. Clint had been surprised when he learned, after knowing him for three months, that he had over a hundred books published. It was a thing called *Enter Merlin Tyana*. The main character was originally based on an Agatha Christie character, Harley Quinn, but that lasted for less than one story, then Merlin took on a mystique of his own. It was certainly no literary masterpiece, but was more readable than most of the crap on the market.

The phone was buzzing when he turned it on in the morning. It was Sergio Sanchez, head of the police.

"Good morning! How are things going, now that you have time to sit around and do nothing?"

"Regular," Clint replied. "How are things with you?"

"Not much changes in Bocas. A different crop of tourists. Different faces, but on the same complainers.

"We have some people over on Bastimentos who are in for a rough time, I'm afraid. Henry and Catherine Dickerson and a few assorted cousins and so forth, for a week or so, at the time. They aren't going to fit. They're on the old Flannery place. George got along with most people here as well as a lot of them over there, but couldn't put up with the ones he didn't like. They stole everything he had, broke into his house a few times, killed his dog – you know about that. He was a basic sort, and not a bad person, at all. Just too hardened in his way.

"These're the type who want to order everyone around them. I mean by that, it's, 'Hand me that fork!' Never a 'please' or 'Thank you' from that crowd. That woman was in the China here. Yveth and Juan were there. She just pointed to her bags and said, 'Bring those to the water taxi!' like they were serfs and she was a princess."

"That one went over pretty big with Yveth, I can guess," Clint said, laughing.

"Yveth looked her right in the eye, and said, 'Portage is twenty five dollars per hour, plus tourist tax, minimum two hours.' She could have sh ... crapped in her panties."

"The Flannery place. Down by that little cove, half a

kilometer from the town? That section isn't where I'd want to be!"

"Or me. I see trouble, ahead. They won't put up with that attitude out there from whatever serves as friends. From gringos? I really don't think so."

They chatted. Clint worked with the police on a number of things. Sergio said there was something about them that had his suspicions on full tilt. He was used to one or two in a family being arrogant egotistical snobs. These were all that way, including the cousins. That said a lot about them, without wasting words.

Clint looked thoughtful, then said he'd call a friend. Maybe they were from somewhere or into something that his friend would know about.

"Ah! That mafia man. Marko. He's living in the Mediterranean, yet still gets that information for you."

"*He*'s living on an island in the Med. His organization's everywhere.

"Do you have any information about them? Where they came from or such?"

"Their passports say they came from New York City. I'm not good at accents. I imagine that you have a lot of them very different in a place like New York. The accents don't fit the name. At all."

"Oh?"

"Dickerson? And an accent that's a lot like some of the French or Suiza."

"It's a name that could be Swiss or Swedish. That area of Europe," Clint pointed out. "I'll see what I can find. Having the US passports says maybe it's witness protection, but they surely wouldn't put them in a place like Bastimentos!"

"That had occurred to me. The US screws up that way all the time. We both have experience with that!"

They chatted a few minutes more about generalities, then Clint called Marko Boccini, a mafia don who had gotten out of the mob business, with Clint's help, and was living with his family on Isla San Cristobal as Manny Mathews. He didn't know anything about them, but would check. It sounded like a typical WPP from the states that was so screwed up it would probably get the whole family wiped out, just by different people than they were being protected from.

Clint went to several places to chat and shop for fresh vegetables, then headed back home. He spent the afternoon in his boat, cruising around. Later, just before dusk fell, he motored up the bay around Bastimentos to look at the house being built on the old Flannery place. It was far too upscale for the area, and as far into crass ostentation. There was a bullish and somewhat fat balding man yelling at the workers. Clint could hear from the distance, when he cut the engine. He was railing about leaving something out to get rained on. Did they have any least idea what that stuff cost? He would take it out of their salaries, if it happened again.

The workers seemed mostly to ignore him. He was yelling mostly in English (which most of them spoke, but they would keep that bit from him), but there were a lot of words mixed in that definitely weren't English.

A tall thin woman came to ask what the yelling was about. It was giving her a headache. They would stop it right now. She was darker than the man, and had a slightly different accent. That would be the one Sergio thought might be French. The man's accent was more guttural.

Clint shook his head and started the engine. The man turned and stared at him. He acted like he didn't even see them as he headed back toward Isla Colon.

That house would be finished soon. The people were staying in the old Flannery house, now. That would be a real move upward to be in the overdone mansion they were building. Flannery had built an ugly wooden stilt house that was old and beginning to deteriorate. Those people were in for a life in hell if they didn't wake up. As soon as the house was finished and there wasn't any work coming from them, they'd get a few lessons in human relations.

Clint was talking to Bob and Aaron at the Golden Grill table a week later. It seemed the Dickerson's house was finished the day before. They were all moving in, today, then the Flannery place was going to be torn down and a gazebo built on the little hill where it stood.

"A what? Here? A gazebo?" Clint asked. "Sergio said they had spent some time in India, probably among the elite English. I can picture a small tiki hut there, but a gazebo?"

"Complete with carved railings and lattice panels," Bob reported. "Rukel's bringing in the special order crap. It's probably soft wood and won't last two days, what with the termites."

"That stuff over to Woodstock? It's supposed to be teak. From Chiriqui." Aaron said. "It won't be there long. Every one of those taxi and tour boats'll end up with, in the vernacular, fancy teakwood appointments."

They chatted about it for a bit, then other subjects. Clint went to the China next door to Rukel and saw the bullish man going in. He grinned to himself and went in to see if they had any anti-fouling paint in yet.

The big man Gloria, the salesgirl, introduced to Clint as Henry Dickerson stood there like a statue and didn't do more than a very short nod.

"Oh, yeah. The new asshole from Bastimentos," Clint replied, with a nod as curt as Dickerson's. "I see the people weren't exaggerating when they said he was an antisocial misfit SOB.

"Any of that Williams Special A-F paint in, yet?" He ignored Dickerson. He'd wanted to see if he could recognize anything about him. Gloria said it was supposed to be shipped Friday, which meant Friday, but probably not this Friday. They laughed about it.

"How in hell...?! You think it's funny that you can't ever get anything on time here?" Dickerson exploded. "Maybe you trash don't care what delays cost, but I *do*! The fact you live like pigs and eat bananas and rice might have something to do with your lack of concern for the costs! I *am* concerned! If you ever had a pot or window, maybe you'd learn some sense about it!"

"Money? Here we go again!" Gloria said, with a sly wink at Clint. "How much it costs to live here where everything's supposed to be so cheap!

"Clint, didn't you get four or five million dollars for that Puerto Armuelles thing?"

Everyone knew how Clint always seemed to end up with ridiculous sums, by accident, in his jobs. He built schools and medical clinics for the Indios and so forth with the money.

"Something like that. I let Judi handle that kind of thing. She's good at seeing most of it isn't stolen. I don't give a happy damn if it is.

"I'll drop in Friday afternoon to see if the A-F is in."

She said her goodbyes, then innocently turned to Dickerson. Clint heard him saying, "That bum has five million dollars?" as he went out. He stopped just outside the door.

"Oh, no. That's just one thing. He has all that land on

the Pacific. He got more than that on several things he did. He really hates having so much, and tries to find ways to make it make a difference for people."

"He's a fool! Money is security!"

"Oh, bullshit! When the market drops or there's a land bust, where is the security?" Gloria said, reasonably. "Your bronze screws are supposed to be on today's truck from David. You paid extra, so they'll be here. About four."

Clint went on, giggling to himself. He did get a lot of money, but nothing nearly like she made it sound. Dickerson would ask a lot of questions about that bum who had a billion dollars in the bank.

He talked to the group at the Golden Grill and to some others. They could have some fun. Then he went home. He would go to Chiriqui Grande in the afternoon, then on to the comarca, then would get back home in two days. Or three. Or four.

Clint tied to his deck and started hauling things inside. Judi waved and said she just had to talk with the mulit-billionaire philanthropist bum who lived next door. He waved back and put his things inside, then went to her place.

" ... So! You got the five plus million for the Puerto Armuelles thing, and were in a land deal out there, too. You had a hundred million or so in that. That thing in Mali, where you got two million back for the Indios, sort of turned into two hundred million. We got carried away, and couldn't stop. I told Manny about it, so he was there at the Lemon Grass with the family for dinner, night before last. I was there with Ben and Gene – he's someone I have to tell you about! I found someone I can really relate to!

"Anyhow, Manny said you were good at ending up with money. You probably got a billion or more from the treasure you found. He knew you started building a huge hospital in some place.

"It was comical! I thought he'd explode!

"I couldn't resist. I said, 'Oh, yeah. Everybody knows Manny spent a few hundred million, himself, building the Isla San Cristobal place. He was in on the school and clinic there with you, wasn't he?' I batted my eyes and looked so innocent you could puke. Sylvia said you two built so many of those things so many places she'd lost count.

"Dick-head-son said it was smarter to conserve some of that money for emergencies. Sylvia said they kept a special account for that. Manny said, 'No, we don't. I kept five million in gold in the vault. You probably do the same.'

"He almost fainted across the table, then I said I only kept fifty thousand around the house. I couldn't picture needing any more than that, and it wouldn't be the end of the world if it was stolen or the house burned down or something.

"He said we sounded like we're a bunch of millionaires. Manny said we just happened to get together here, that it was a strange place, that way – the people you meet here.

"People came by all the time. I think Flora told them to say big hellos. Dickerson and his wife gave her trouble every time they came in. We had six or eight come over to ask all about you and us. We hugged them all. They all acted like big super-mogul Henry wasn't even there."

"What does he do – other than be an obnoxious ass?" Clint asked, giggling.

"That's about it, I guess. He says he owned some company in New York. I acted like the last thing I wanted to hear was how some silly two-bit egomaniac got his pitiful little stash. Manny will know."

They chatted about more pleasant things for an hour or so. Clint caught up on all the local happenings, then he went back to his place and caught up with his e-mail and such, then called Manny.

"He was a stockbroker, with his own company. He liquified before he came here, according to information. Something over six million dollars.

"He's terribly impressed with money. Judi got us started. We all ended up worth several hundred billion. She said she only kept fifty grand or so around the house, for emergencies. That wouldn't be enough to notice if somebody took it."

"According to information?"

"He didn't own that company. It closed because Harold Didrickson was dying of cancer."

"WP?"

"That's the strange part of it. Definitely and positively, no. He was in on some things, at the fringes, with some big families in York. There was nothing that would put him onto witness protection. He was just a puppet they used in several ways. He probably cleared about thirty grand a year and some expenses. Now he's here with six million in the bank?"

"Well, so long as he keeps it to himself, who cares," Clint said. "Why was he with you at the Lemon Grass, at all?"

"His wife, Cathy-dear, had met Judi. They happened to come in as we did. They inserted themselves. We got rid of them when Judi said she had to go. They didn't have much choice. They left, too."

"Contrived?"

"Obviously. Judi said she ran into her at the garden club. There're not ten people in the world less interested in gardening than Cathy-honey."

They talked a bit, then Clint rang off. The Dickersons were most probably just some pains-in-the-asses with delusions, who were trying to find a place they'd fit. They'd inherited – or stole – a lot of money.

Clint's nutty botanist/musician friend, Dave, came by. He asked why Xavier Franconi was in town, asking about new people in the area. Did he think no one here would know who he was?

"Who is he?" Clint asked.

"Oh, right. The music. He was a sort of front man for some of those formula bands the mobs put together in the mid-eighties. Sort of a muscle/security chief."

"Which mob? Not California, surely!"

"Somebody operating out of Motown. That's where that kind of crap started. One or two made it pretty big, most flopped out after a year or so."

They talked about the comarca and their mutual Indio friends. Dave got along with the Indios as well as Clint.

Later, Clint went over to the Rip Tide for talk and a couple of draft beers, then went into town for awhile, met a girl from New Zealand, and had a very pleasant night.

"Clint? Sergio here."

"Yo?" Clint answered the phone while laying on his hammock on the deck, drinking coffee. Laura had just left to get back to her group before they woke up, so they wouldn't know she wasn't at the hotel last night.

"Remember the Dickerson people? On Bastimentos?"

"I'd like to forget. What's up?"

"A cousin, Danny Lesterinni, is dead. It looks like their neighbors have had enough of them. I'm going out. Care to come along?"

Clint considered, decided he couldn't care less, remembered what Dave said about possible mob connections and what Manny said about him not being anybody important to any mob.

"I'll come over. We can take my boat."

"I already sent the big boat. I'll be on the dock."

Clint threw on some clothes (he didn't wear anything until he decided what he was going to do on a given day) and headed for the police dock. Sergio was waiting. They headed for Bastimentos.

"It seems this Lesterinni was as popular among the people out here as the rest of them. He was chopped up pretty well. I think, maybe, from what they told me over the phone, he was tortured with a machete until he bled to death. We won't know until Doc gives a verdict."

Clint nodded. He maneuvered into the overdone dock with it's nispero, teak, and cedar gear house on the end. Sergio looked at it and shook his head. He hadn't been closer than in the bay, out a distance, where very little could be seen of the house. He shook his head again at the view from the dock of the overdone ostentation.

"Loads of class," he remarked. "Too bad it's all mud-bottom low." Clint grinned.

Victor met them at the fancy dock and said he had some serious questions about that body.

"Oh? What kind of questions?" Sergio asked of his sergeant.

"How some of those cuts were supposed to have been made with a machete, not a fileting knife. How he got those burns all over his body from any machete. Mainly, why anybody would report it was done with a machete."

"The person who called, a Julia Bianco, said it looked like he was chopped up with a machete. She probably wouldn't know the difference. She was hysterical," Sergio replied.

"Oh. Well, he's over there (pointing to a little gazebo. It seemed they didn't build a gazebo, after all. They built three)."

They walked over to check out the scene. It was gory. Clint noticed the blood spatter patterns and smirked at Sergio and Victor.

"Yeah," Sergio suggested. "He was dead before he was tortured. It would appear someone wants us to think he was tortured." Clint nodded his agreement.

"There's a lot strange about this one," Victor said. "This looks like something set up on a movie lot. Someone wants us to think the Indios did it, or the blacks. The Indios wouldn't do anything like that, while the blacks would have done a lot of different things, but not like that."

"It's like a stage setting," Sergio replied.

Clint remembered what Bob said at the Golden Grill. "That's for dead certain," he remarked.

They went on to the house, when Doc came over in the hospital boat. He'd taken one look, and said, "They think we don't know anything about CSI? Surely they don't think we'll fall for something this obvious!"

"They would in New York," Clint replied. "If they paid the right person, it would already be marked as an unsolvable case. It was, more than obviously, racially motivated. A hate crime with fifty thousand suspects in the area and no clues that would point in any direction."

"There are only about a thousand, here," Sergio pointed out. Clint gave him the finger.

Dickerson and his wife were sitting with three people in the large overdone salon. The women were huddled in one area, the men in another. The room was like a big dance hall, complete with a wet bar on one side.

"Cheap casino elegance," Victor mumbled to Clint, who nodded. "Well, they're casino-type people," he answered.

Sergio got the names and passport copies and such from each of them, asked a few questions, and said he'd be back later, when the ME finished his CSI.

"You have a ME and CSI team?" Catherine, the wife, asked, looking a bit nervous and scared.

"Certainly!" Victor said. "We're not really in the eighteen fifties here. We have to send a lot of things to Panamá City for analysis, but we have as modern a lab as anyone."

They moved around the house and asked very few questions. Clint was cornered by Dickerson and asked how long the investigation would take. He had to go to the states for three days, soon.

"It takes as long as it takes," Clint answered. "They're efficient."

"I can't believe they'd actually do anything like that!" he cried. "I know they hate us, but I didn't think they'd do anything like *that*!"

"They who?" Clint asked, innocently.

"The Indios, or those niggers, of course! Who else would do anything like that?"

"Who else, indeed?" Clint agreed. "Trouble is, it's as plain as the overdone house here that none of them did it. One glance told us that."

"Oh? You're an expert at that, too?" he spat.

"Yup! Full qualifications from Florida, the US, here ... it's my business."

"Er! I didn't ever ask what your business is?"

"Investigator. Private and official."

"They never told ... I mean, you must have an interesting ... I mean, it's, er, good to know they have somebody here who knows his ass from a cowflop with this kind of thing."

Clint had to turn away to hide that he was trying not to laugh out loud. Dickerson was definitely not prepared to meet anyone who knew anything whatever about murder investigation.

"We'll have some questions, later," he said. "We have to know what to ask. We'll have to get background information on all of you. Routine to know everything you can about suspects."

"Er."

Clint went back to Sergio. He said he wanted information about this bunch of rich thugs, bimbos, and trailer trash.

"Manny, there's something to do with some mob connections here, it seems" Clint said. "These people wouldn't fit with anyone else. They're trying to put on a face like they've been around the world and are sophisticated and elite. They've probably never been outside of ... Dave said Motown."

"I have a contact there. Jefferson. Used to be mob, went legit the last few ... Wait! That's Cleveland. Greco's in Motown."

"Mo Jefferson? I met him in Florida. I think I also met Greco ... Miklokaras there, too. I kind of liked Greco. I was totally neutral about Mo."

"I can get some info from them, if they have it. Sylvia says she thinks she's seen one of those women. Women who hang around their mansion in Carmel.

"What's going on? I heard somebody got butchered by the Indios."

"It was supposed to look like that."

"I see."

Clint remembered what Dave said. "What do you know about a Xavier Franconi?"

"Cheap wannabe hanging around the music business, then into art and jewelry theft. Not worth troubling about."

"Even if he's here, in Bocas?"

There was a long pause. "I think I want to know some things. I'll keep you informed."

Clint thanked him and hung up.

What could it be? If Manny said they weren't witness protection, what were they? If they were trying to hide, why the ostentation?

Clint decided to go fishing. It was the last thing those people would expect of him.

Clint was tying to his deck when he heard his phone buzz. He'd forgotten it. Again.

It quit before he got to it. There was a notation that he had 23 missed calls. He checked his incoming and found Judi, Sergio, and Manny had called him. Repeatedly.

Manny first: "Clint, there's some weird kind of complete silence in an area there never is. I can't find out what's going on here. Mention Xavier Franconi in passing or something when they're around."

"This is somehow connected with the mobs, then?"

"Yeah, Clint. I just can't get a hint as to how."

They talked, then Clint called Judi, who said Manny and Sergio were trying to contact him. She didn't know why, but it was urgent.

Sergio said he was in the police boat, headed for Bastimentos. There was a lot about those people that didn't click – such as that Lesterinni had had extensive plastic surgery. Such as at least one of them had a phony passport. Such as the business Dickerson was supposed to have sold was never his to sell.

Clint said he'd get over as fast as he could, which was fast, with his boat. He hung up and headed for Bastimentos. Sergio was standing on the dock, talking with Victor, when Clint pulled up a few minutes later. They waited. Clint said he wanted to try something to see if they could get a reaction. Victor said that Cathy-sweetheart hinted about bribing him, but he let her know there wasn't a chance.

"Sergio, get DNA samples from all of them."

"They'll refuse."

"They don't know the law here. Just tell them Doc is going to take samples, so line up."

Sergio grinned. He said that might light a fire or two!

They went to the house. They did know that about the law. Sergio raised an eyebrow.

"Well, I suppose that means you can take them all to the lockup," Clint suggested. "The law says they don't have to volunteer, but that not volunteering shows they have something to hide, so you can hold them for investigation for as long as six months. I'm sure they'll leave a sample or two around in that amount of time."

"Er, can I speak with you privately, Faraday?" Dickerson asked.

Clint went out on the verandah with him and his wife.

"We can't allow this!" he cried. "My god! This is impossible! We can't let these people dig around in our past! We have to have full privacy. We came here because we heard there was no place in the world where you could have as much privacy as here!"

"Up to a point. Murder suspects don't get privacy anywhere, when they refuse to cooperate."

"But ... I swear, we didn't have anything to do with any murder here!" Cathy cried.

"Here? Then why go through all this crap?"

"I guess we don't have a choice," Cathy said. "No, dear. We have to do it.

"You see, Mr. Faraday, we're on the witness protection plan in the states, in Oklahoma. We're witnesses in a big trial about stock fraud, where we were threatened. Two people were already killed by those people. We don't know what to do. We didn't know how much trouble we would get into, or we wouldn't have ever agreed to anything. I think they've found us. I think we'll all end up dead, if we can't get away from here!"

"Plus, these people will kill us in a blink!" Dickerson said. "They hate us because we're more, er, civilized.

They're jealous and violent. I don't think the people in Kansas, er, Oklahoma have found us. It was the niggers, here."

"If you go to any place in the world and act like asshole snobs, you'll be resented. The Indios don't hate you, they pity you. Your lives are nothing but fear, greed, and false fronts. The blacks won't do anything other than try to make life so miserable you'll leave. That's what happened to Flannery, the one here before you."

"They are certainly *not* our kind of people," Cathy complained. "They have no breeding. They're savages!"

"They have a hell of a lot more breeding than any of you. They couldn't care less how much money you stole somewhere else. They're exactly what you see. You are, too. You just don't realize that it's so obvious to them that you're what they call 'trailer trash' in the states. You've never been anywhere and never made an honest buck in your lives, now you pay the price.

"I think one or more of you killed Lesterinni and tried to make it look like a hate killing. Either that, or some-one like Franconi."

"*Wha..!!* What do you know about Franconi?!" Dickerson almost screamed. Cathy-darlin' looked like she'd been slapped in the puss with a rotten fish. She said, "How do you even know about ... the name, Franconi? He's a cheap hood in, er, Arkansas. He was going to tell the ... go to ... someplace. Some people."

"He's a cheap hood right here in Bocas Town, at the moment. We checked on his type, first thing."

"He's in Bocas?! Oh, dear god! We're dead! All of us! He's a professional killer for the mob in Chicago!"

"Make up your mind. He's a second-rate thug from Motown, not from Oklahoma or Kansas or Arkansas,"

Clint replied. "Why do you think – this is eighteen hundred and these are hicks from Podunk investigating your little murder? These guys are more efficient than most places in the states.

"You can give me a straight story, or I can dig it up. It's what I do. Each one of you who ends up dead tells me a little more."

Sergio came out and asked Clint if he should arrest the lot of them for further questioning, or would they cooperate. Clint replied that they weren't legal. They were here hiding from someone who, apparently, found them.

"Well, I don't think more than eighty percent of the gringos living here are legal. I don't care, so long as they stay out of trouble and don't bring this kind of thing here. I can't protect anybody who doesn't even tell me what they have to be protected *from*. That's asking far too much.

"Clint, you've always come through for the Policia Nacional here. You've donated millions of dollars, billions (Judi told him about that), to the Indios and everybody else. We deeply respect you for being a true, caring person. I will act on your advice, here."

"Okay. Let it ride – for now. I have to check on a thing or two. One person in Bocas Town seems connected. He may be our killer, but he may not be."

"Fair enough. If you wish to return to Bocas I will cadge a ride with you. The investigation boat will be here for another hour or so.

"We can go in about ten minutes." Sergio went back inside.

"Just like that? You have enough influence to control these people, just like that?"

"I don't control anybody. I respect them, they respect

me. Life's a lot easier for that.

"I'll check on Franconi. I'll try to get him to decide he'd like to see Panamá City or David or something. He'd fit in certain sections there. Maybe Colon, but he'd live maybe a day there, if his attitude's anything like yours. I'll be in touch." He walked inside to signal to Sergio that he was ready to go. They headed back to Bocas Town. Clint wanted to know a thing or two about Franconi. The reaction was expected to be a little shock or something. It was far too much.

Franconi was sitting on the deck at The Reef, having a beer and chicken and rice. Clint slid in across from him. He looked up, grinned, and said, "Faraday, isn't it?"

"Yeah. What's up with that bunch of obnoxious trailer trash on Bastimentos that's so important you had to kill one of them?"

He laughed. "I haven't killed anybody. I don't know what's going on with the cruds. All I'm supposed to do is hang around to keep an eye on them. I work for a group who ... I don't know what it's about, only that they have to be watched until some kind of solution can be found to the problem, whatever it is. If I'm to contact them or anything, I'll get orders.

"It's not the kind of thing I do. I don't like being here. I made some bad moves when I came and got too many people against me. I acted like this is Chicago or LA. Stupid as all hell! I *know* better!"

"Now it's LA, too? I learn things."

"Lucerne and Bianco are from the area. I'm not drunk or running my mouth or anything. I was told, in no uncertain terms that I was to level with you, if you got involved. Some people concerned have been burned by you, before."

"I know who Bianco is. Lucerne?"

"Frank Lucerne. Another cousin – or whatever they're supposed to be."

"What are they?"

"Besides some used-to-be hangers on, I don't know. I think they have something that belongs to someone. They've already gotten more than seven million dollars from him. They spend it on cheap crap they think is classy – like that sick monstrosity they built on Bastimentos. Just supposition, but I think it's something that gets used if certain ones of them get dead. It's what's keeping them alive. Those people don't fool around with that shit. They put a permanent end to it."

"Then Lesterinni was just there, basically, because he didn't have any other possible out."

"I think he was looking for a possible way out for more than three years. He doesn't look like he did, back then. He was seeing some people he wasn't supposed to be seeing. I know that, because I was told he went to the FBI offices on the sly, twice, when he thought he'd given some people the slip.

"He did give one of them the slip, but there were others with the same assignment."

"Probably where the WP idea came from."

"They told you they were on WP?"

"Yeah. From Arkansas, Kansas, and Oklahoma."

"Then you know three places you needn't bother to check. None of them were ever in those places. Ever, ever, ever." He laughed.

"Obvious, like everything else they do.

"Look. Don't kill anyone here. I'll tag you. We don't need anymore hits here. Let them hit each other."

"Hmm. You know something." It was a statement that sounded like a statement.

"Somebody said the wrong thing."

He nodded. Clint said to enjoy Bocas. He went back to his place. He had something more to check.

"Manny, there's some kind of huge connection. I think Lesterinni was going to the FBI and had plastic surgery at their expense to use in the WP."

"I can't get information from some people from New York, LA, Cleveland, and Detroit. It's big," Manny replied. "We dug into Franconi a lot deeper. He's a lot more professional than we thought. He's smart. He makes it appear he's just a runner or cheap muscle man, so no one pays him much attention."

"I talked with him. He has instructions to level with me."

"Doniletti? I really don't think so! Mo Jefferson or Miklokaras? It doesn't fit. They're legitimate now, and don't worry about such crap anymore. I have to see if there's someone on the way up who has too much to lose."

"Manny, check on someone who's been around a long time and keeps a very low profile."

"You know something, Clint? I think I want to check on people who have dealings with the mobs, but who aren't directly involved. Maybe politicians or big business CEOs. Or whatever."

"With what was going on – and probably still is – with Bush, I think maybe that's a very real possibility. I hadn't considered it."

"You never thought of the mobs and the top pols together before Bush. Not to a great extent. Local and state contracts with them for roads or garbage or whatever. Nobody knows how that works better than me! Now it's right there in the White House. All Haliburton ever was is a mob connection, in my

opinion. There's no big secret who was their represen-
tative in the White house.

"It started a long time ago, with the military and drug
deals and such. It's gotten so that the entire system is
rotted clear through. I can say that one good thing about
Old Pop. He made the people around him his first
consideration. He impressed on me my whole life that
we were in a position to save a lot for our people. It was
us or something one hell of a lot worse."

"You might be able to unearth something with that
approach. I'll do what digging I can from this end."

They chatted a few minutes. When they broke it off,
Clint sat back to consider things. It did have a political
stench about it, in some ways. His connection was
through Franconi and that bunch on Bastimentos. If he
could find who they really were he could find who and
what was behind the whole scheme.

He made a few more calls, then went back to the
computer. He first checked on the major political
connections in Detroit. That was where it came from, so
far as he knew.

After three hours he had a lot of nothing. He sat back
to think again, then wondered: If this came from Detroit,
would these people be talking about Detroit? Would
they have those addresses on their papers?

That left him with a big blank. No one in New York or
Chicago would say anything to Manny, which probably
meant they didn't know anything. Where was any little
clue to give him a home base? None of them had
dropped the name of the actual place. They wouldn't.

Manny's wife had seen one of them in Carmel. Would
it be ...? He called Manny. That was one thing he was
checking from the angle of some politician or business
head there. He would have answers in about two hours.

He would call Clint. It would be a large business or top politician.

Clint thought again, then had what might give him a clue, or might not. He walked into town and to the police station to have Sergio get some things for him. From the property registers and from a bank. And from a lawyer, if they could find which one.

Sergio sent a man to the court to get a demanda form, then handed it to Clint and told him to go over to Changuinola. All the registrations were there.

Clint took the water taxi to Almirante, then the bus from there to Changuinola. He presented the court demanda to the woman at the public registry and received the entire paperwork on the Bastimentos property from the time Flannery bought it from Shepard Robinson Puenta until today.

He went through the papers and had copies made of six pages, at his expense, $3.21. When he left the registry he caught a quick glimpse of a person in a cab and grinned to himself. What he wanted might actually be in those papers!

He then took the papers back to Bocas Town. Manny called to say there was a bit of a stir in Carmel. He didn't know who, but knew it was someone there. Any hint, he could locate their man. Clint said he'd call back in an hour or so, if he found anything, then told Manny what he'd done. He took the papers to his house, where he spent some time studying them.

The lawyer was with a local firm. The bank used was Citicorps, in Panama', and LA International Trust Reserve, in the states. That, at least, made it fairly certain the main connection was there.

Clint thought a bit, then sighed. He went to Martin, Martin, Strent and Arauz, Abogados, and talked with

Lorenzo Martin. He handled the transfers and so forth. He knew about the murder. He would cooperate as much as was legal. He didn't know much, past that a man had come with Dickerson with a certified check from the states that he had taken his fees from when they paid for the property. He had a copy of the check in the files, no one said anything about not showing it to the police, Clint represented the police. He had produced a court order, proving it.

It was just a cashier's check. There wasn't a signature or mention who it came from. It was for one million US dollars. Martin had arranged for direct deposit transfer in Citicorp Bank in David, with his fees taken out the moment the transfer was cleared. It's three days wait for a certified cashier's check from the states. The transfer cost them $3,400.

Clint wrote down the number of the check, thanked Martin, and went back to the police station. Sergio couldn't get information from any bank in LA.

Clint called Manny to give him the number. It was less than twenty minutes later when Manny called. He said the check was bought by a large company with an account there. It may be an Italian company. Napoli Diversified.

Clint went back home, fixed dinner, cleaned up, and went back into town. Manny called. "Arno Napoli has a company in LA that doesn't seem to have a product or service on the market, yet it takes in several million per year. They pay taxes on that much. My dead ends keep running into dead ends on that company and Napoli."

They chatted a bit, then Clint rung off. He knew a lot now, but not what he needed.

Clint saw Franconi sitting in the parque, talking to a girl. He went by and said, "Good evening. I see I'm you new job."

Franconi laughed. "Yes. You have some dangerous and influential people busting their asses trying to keep you from finding out who they are."

"Tell Napoli I know who he is. There's no way to keep that much money from getting attention."

Franconi laughed again, and saluted. Clint went to the Toro Loco for a couple of cold Balboas and some mingling, then went home. He didn't quite know where to go with this, now. He had to discover what was going on with Dickerson and company. Knowing who he had something on didn't help a lot if you didn't know what it was.

It was time to consider different angles on this stupid thing. Why Panamá? Why not the islands near Panamá City? That was where the ostentation wouldn't be so much out of place. Why not Rio? That was the kind of place they would fit a bit better than anywhere in Panamá. Islands? There were some hundreds of them where those people would fit better, though the type wouldn't fit well anywhere.

Was that an act, for some reason? Why make your-selves unpopular to the point no one would question if you got knocked over?

Looked at that way, they didn't come – they were sent. Somebody wanted them placed where they could be eliminated without a lot of comment or investigation.

Take it on: they were sent to where they could be removed, but sending them cost one hell of a lot of money. That left only one logical reason. Blackmail. They had the "insurance" with them. They probably also had it spread around with some system where it would be delivered to someone or some organization in the case where they were knocked over.

So. When whatever part Lesterinni had in it was neutralized he was eliminated as a problem, here, where there was the chance that, done right, it wouldn't be investigated much.

No one could take that chance. His killer was one of them. That left that they were set up in a way they could be gotten rid of. It still didn't add up.

Clint was going to have to meet the other players. He knew the Dickersons well enough that he could say they had a degree of fear that told him they didn't have any connection with his murder. Directly. All of them were connected.

He went to town, where he found Franconi at the Golden Grill. He asked for a minute. He was waved into a seat. "Which one of them did Lesterinni?" he asked.

"You don't think it was me?"

"Not a chance. Messy, which you're not, as well as unprofessional, which you're not."

"I think Lucerne, but it could be Herman."

"You have a clue what it's about? Other than the obvious. I mean what they base the blackmail on."

He didn't blink. He shook his head.

"They've gone a long time without drawing attention to themselves. This was a big blunder. I think Napoli, at least, knows that."

He nodded, and replied, "There's no 'them'."

Clint nodded and bought them both Balboas. They chatted for half an hour or so, then Clint headed back home. He called Manny to tell him what he thought. Manny agreed.

"Oh. One other little item I've learned. We can stop referring to them."

"Them who?"

"It's 'him', not 'them'."

"Sure?"

"Pretty much."

"Then he's going to get the investigation he set this up to avoid."

"I think so. I want to know what this is about. I think Panamá's being used because there's something here."

"Laundering," Manny said. "Panamá makes that easy, with the off-shores and so forth."

"Maybe not laundering. Just the fact that he has those offshores. I wish I knew even enough to get some information as to how much – in a general sense."

"It'll be big."

"I think so."

He had a direction, if it was the wrong one. He still had to meet the others. Frieda Herman and Frank Lucerne. That would leave Julia Bianco to complete the roster at that house. Clint got in his boat and headed out to Bastimentos. Maybe he could make one of them slip so he would know who butchered Lesterinni.

The whole bunch were on the dock, arguing with the officer there. Dickerson saw Clint coming in. He called that the damned cops wouldn't let them take a trip over to David for a couple of days.

"A couple of days? You have enough luggage stacked up there to go to David for twenty years," Clint replied. "I'll try to clear this up so you can skip, but you won't get far, if you run. Where would you go?"

"I don't think we have to worry about whoever killed Danny," Frieda Herman said. "He brought it on himself. He would actually go into town by himself! These people hate us! He knew it was dangerous!"

"Nobody from Bastimentos killed him," Clint said, sourly. "I have to talk with you, all of you. Privately."

"You ain't talking to none of me!" Dickerson spat. "I said all I know!"

"Okay! Your choice!" Clint replied. "When you want this cleared up to where you can get off the island, let me know."

"Hey!" Dickerson yelled.

Clint waved and started his engine. He dropped it into reverse.

"Wait! What the holy *hell*!" Dickerson wailed. "I only meant I don't know nothing! I ain't got nothing I *can* tell you!"

"Get off the attitude or you'll be here until you die of old age – if any of you live to be old."

"We'll talk to you, if we have to," Catherine said, defeatedly. "I can't stay cooped up here much longer. I'm going stir crazy! All the TV has is in Spanish. There's not even any good music or anything on the radio. I can't *stand* this much longer!"

"I don't know what you need, but I'll give it a go," Frank Lucerne said. "Walk around the place and talk, or the boathouse?"

"I can fish off the dock here. I like to fish," Dickerson said. "Ever body else can go away for two minutes while I tell you everthing I know."

"We all like to fish," Julia agreed. "That's one of the main reasons we agreed, uh, why we came here."

"Okay. We can go out in my boat and fish while we talk," Clint suggested. "Right around the point there are some coral heads. The fishing's really good."

Julia didn't say anything. She went into the boathouse and came out with a tackle box and a rod and reel. She climbed into the boat, and said, "Drive on, Jeeves!"

Clint grinned and backed out. He went around the point and anchored between two colorful coral heads. They could see the mangrove and yellow-tail snapper around the reef. They baited and dropped their lines.

"Which one of you offed Danny?" he asked, bluntly.

"God! I wish I knew! I wish I knew *why*!"

"What do you have on Napoli?"

She studied him for a few seconds. "I have some pictures of him with people he definitely doesn't want to be seen around. It could cause all kind of problems for him with another bunch. They're digital and printed. The pictures. They're in a place where nobody will see them, so long as nobody bugs me or ... anything."

"They found how to stop whatever Danny had. It put all of you in danger. One or more of you knocked him over."

"Probably. It wasn't me." She got a bite and fought a large corvel into the boat. She asked Clint if they ate them here. They didn't where she came from. Alabama, right above Pensacola, Florida. She grew up there until she was 17.

Clint told her how to prepare them so they were delicious. He told her to bleed them while they were alive so the oils in the blood wouldn't ruin the meat. She took a fileting knife from he tackle box to cut off the tail like he suggested and hung it over the side.

He caught a snapper and threw it back. He said he had plenty in his freezer.

They went back to the dock. Frank Lucerne was waiting with his gear. He got in the boat. Clint went to a spot not far from the first, and anchored. Lucerne had much the same answers as Julia. He was from Baton Rouge, Louisiana, and had gone to Hollywood to be an actor.

"I was always the type women go for. I thought that would make me a super star in a week. I was an idiot! I worked in a restaurant and as a meatcutter to eat. Good thing my Pops was a butcher. I had a trade. I did get in a couple of flicks, but they were mostly just hotrods and ass. I was somebody the women flirted with. They could show off their tits and asses with me."

Clint had seen the type in those movies. No talent, just another prop for background.

Frank caught two snapper. He said this was a good idea. Each one of them could catch their own supper. He didn't delude himself into thinking they were going anywhere soon. They wouldn't have made it out of the country and would just make themselves look guilty. He wasn't bothered much by the murder. He never did like Lesterinn. They didn't have much in common.

"Hmm. What do you have on Napoli?" Clint asked. Lucerne looked shocked for a second, then grinned. "Nothing he can stop. It's up to him whether or not it stays with me."

"How did the bunch of you get together? Screw Napoli club?"

"Sort of. He was a little worried, because we all had something, and didn't even know each other. He said we could find a place somewhere where he could keep tabs on us and he would give us each a million dollars. He named a few places he said were like paradise. We went to a place in Mexico, then Nicaragua, then here. He knew we all liked fishing. He just sent us where the fishing was good and the place was really nice. We really like it here, but we don't fit. Henry and Danny are the worst. I can get along anywhere, but he started it, so the people don't like us. I can't change their ideas. Frieda and I can get along. The others are what we call rednecks. They think they can order anyone around they like because they're millionaires. It don't work here. Catherine has an attitude. She tries to flirt with the guys, but that won't cut it. They as much as tell her to fuck herself, if she wants to fuck."

"That's about what I figured." Clint went back and picked up Frieda. Much the same. She had audio CDs and memory sticks. The way they kept the information made it really bad for Napoli if anything happened to her.

She caught a black sea bass. She agreed with Frank that they could all catch their own supper. They didn't cook for each other, except sometimes her and Frank, who wasn't a bad guy.

She cleaned the fish right there, and threw the guts, bones, and fins overboard. She was fast and made very good filets, with minimal waste.

The Dickersons wanted to come together. Clint agreed. He said he knew they had their story worked out together, so nothing was lost. He wasn't going to put up with the arrogant asshole act.

They were subdued and scared. They were afraid Napoli had sent someone to kill them off, one at the time. He'd seen a man who he saw with Napoli in LA walking around right there in Bocas Town.

"Franconi? I know him. I talked with him."

"He told you about us and Napoli?"

"No. He doesn't talk about that kind of thing. Ever. Anywhere. Under any conditions."

"What the hell did he carve Danny up like that for?!" Catherine wailed. "If he was just supposed to kill him, why do that?"

"He didn't kill him. He's professional. It would be fast and clean." Clint said.

"Oh, dear god! Then there's someone else?" Catherine cried, wide-eyed.

"Someone not professional? Maybe it really was some nigger," Dickerson said. "Maybe we got our shorts in knots over nothin'! I'll be dog-damned!"

"Well, if you're going to demean people like that, I suppose you have to expect that someday you'll insult the wrong one and pay the price," Clint replied.

"I hate nights here," Catherine wailed. "Henry drinks a few beers and can sleep through an atomic attack. I need a quart of tequila and still can't sleep long. Oh, I *hate* this place!"

"C'est la vie," Clint replied.

They didn't catch anything. Clint gave them a large yellow snapper he caught for their supper. Dickerson asked if he could arrange for them to go to David for a few days. Catherine said there wasn't any point. It wasn't from Napoli. She never really thought it was. He had too much to lose. They never carried cash. These people would murder them all for fifty dollars. They could get the cash from any ATM. They could get enough for the plane at the airport, or they could stop at the national bank. It had a Clave machine. It was on the way.

Clint explained there weren't flights to Bocas Town from David anymore. There wasn't really a reason to run.

"It might hit the fan because somebody else snuffed him, though," Dickerson suggested. "It still means the stuff he had gets out."

"What do you have?" Clint asked.

"No comment!" he fired back. Clint grinned. He dropped them off at the dock and talked to the officer there to say they couldn't go anywhere with luggage for more than a night or two.

"But they're millionaires. They can buy all that stuff, anywhere," he replied.

"That leaves a trail others can follow. They don't have cash. They use the ATMs."

Clint went back home. He had hoped to get some kind of clue about Lesterinni, but they all were expert with a fileting knife. He did get confirmation that he knew what was going on. He just didn't have a clue as to why. He wondered greatly why Danny Lesterinni was dead.

Manny had reached a dead end with Napoli. He said that would have worried him a couple of years ago, but he didn't care. He didn't need to try to keep up with those states mobsters. He had enough in untraceable accounts that he could totally disappear from the world. Marko Boccini was dead and gone, so far as the world knew. He was a totally different person. He was a family man with a beautiful wife and two great kids. His kids could wear the name, "Mathews," that would get true respect for their father, not fear.

"Okay. What happened?" Clint asked.

"Nothing, really, and everything. I woke up this morning, when the baby gave its five thirty wake-up call. Sylvia made me some coffee made from beans from right here, with a little chocolate mixed in that was also from this place, and some natural brown sugar, grown right here. There were those fishcakes Judi taught her to make, from fish I caught off my own dock, right here, and some patacones from plantains, from right here. The sunrise would blow your mind.

"Anyhow, I was in the kitchen washing up my own dishes and thinking like I talk now. I understood right at that moment that the cheap two-bit gringo hood, Marko Boccini, mafia don, was dead and gone. The not-so-bad Panamanian, Manny Mathews, was alive and kicking.

"God! What a feeling! I never knew before how true what you said when we met was. I'm *free*! Nobody owns me! I don't answer to anybody. Nobody and no money owns me, anymore. No matter how much money I got, I was still that cheap two-bit hood.

"Clint, I was never responsible for anything, before.

Now, I'm responsible for my family and friends – and, most of all, for *me*!

"See, it didn't matter what I did before. It wasn't my fault. It was the way of the world, or Joe Blow, or sex on TV, or whatever. I was a damned slave to that life and didn't know it. The song Dave sang the other night said what it really is. The line, 'the freedom *of* my chains,' is a *fact*!"

"Your first religious experience, and you're not religious."

"That's just another form of slavery. Anyhow, I don't care about that stuff anymore. For real. Anytime I use those old connections it'll be to help the normal Joe.

"What made me see it was looking for that Napoli character. I just, all-at-once, saw how he's a slave on the run from himself. I'm like your – our – Indio friends. I pity him. Probably a billion dollars cash, still a slave with no way out.

"I found my way out. All it took was one true friend. Thanks for being that friend."

They chatted awhile. Clint had watched the change from one of the world's most powerful and feared mobsters to Manny Mathews, the regular nice guy living over on San Cristobal. He saw it in him when he first came to Panamá. He'd known his father, in the states, had done a favor for him (he still didn't know what that favor was) and had a vow that anything Clint ever needed was his for a word. That promise carried to his son. Clint saw the longing for a decent life in Marko's eyes when he was here. He helped him establish the new identity.

That still left him with a wonder of why any of this happened.

"Manny, what has he done that makes him so afraid of

being found now? Do you even have an idea?"

"That life. He feels like he had it made. He's worth millions or even billions. Nobody ever knew it was crooked. He feels like he's been more clever than anyone else in the whole damned country. He managed to screw all of them in one way or another, and never got caught at it. Now there's someone or something that can bring it all out. Probably everyone around him thinks he's a great person who beat the odds.

"It's about reputation and respect. He did it all for respect, same as I did. The real difference is, nobody actually respected me, they were all scared shitless of me. I didn't have real respect to lose. He does, but it's a lie, and he knows it. The most important thing in the world is that no one ever knows.

"I'll bet another thing. He probably has kids by a couple of women, but never loved anyone in his life. That means no one ever loved him. That means it's all for nothing. Respect is the only thing he has. He'd lose everything else in the world to keep that respect."

"That's a cold psychological argument that's probably right on the money. Depending on what he's done, I might try to arrange that he doesn't lose the respect if I can find out what it's about."

"He'd be smarter to blow his brains out before it comes out, probably. He will, if it comes out."

"Maybe he deserves that, too. I pity the type. That's real."

A few minutes later they said their "Good lucks!" and hung up. Clint wanted to know what Napoli was hiding from. When it came to killing even such as Lesterinni it had gone too far. That he had arranged that was pretty clear. The look of torture about it was a warning to the rest of them. "Shut up and stay shut up or...."

Clint also wanted to know which one was so cold-blooded he or she could continue the act so easily. That was going to take some digging. He had three suspects. There was something ... there always was.

Now that he had a complete name and the company name he could use the computer to trace a lot about him. There was simply no way to keep everything off the net. Sometimes it seemed like there was no way to keep *anything* off the net. You don't have to worry about Big Brother watching you, you have to worry about everyone and his dog watching you.

Clint sat at the computer and brought up Google Search. He tagged everywhere he wanted to go on that, then brought up Yahoo! Search. He repeated it with lesser-known search engines. Four hours later he had a starting point, so perked a large pot of coffee and started on it. He would take Napoli Diversified (that had now grown to Napoli Diversified Investments and Services, Ltd/SA).

The company mostly made recommendations for investments. It seemed to have a good streak of luck, after being in business for four years, when it found a client who wanted to invest in international development of business and real estate. It suddenly showed a profit of four point two million dollars in the last five months of 1986, nine million for 1987, twenty one million for 1988, etc. There was some question of one client who seemed to be selling a lot of things more than he could account for. He was investigated for fraud, but nothing was found. The investments were in other countries. The money sent to the states after being banked in several other countries for a certain period. When the accounts reached a certain point, the money was transferred to LA banks. In 1989 the accounts were consolidated into a single international bank account, meaning that fees were cut in half, or more. The records were then open to the proper agencies. investigations showed it was all legitimate when sent to the US branches.

Clint spent seven hours tracing money for that client. He found that, once the international bank was used and the accounts simply transferred to other branches, the source of the money wasn't watched much at all.

He played it close to the line until he shifted the attention to movements, not sources. It was laundered, probably from drugs.

Napoli had cut himself into it with the origination of the scheme: very likely. He then handled the accounts of more and more such sources until he ended up with a cut of a major part of the drug supply business. He was known as a very liberal spender for causes, and was helping several hundred local people with scholarships and medical and so forth. It was all in his local community, not far from Carmel, California. He was also known as a person who was "No tolerance!" with drug dealers, and for spending excessively large sums for rehabilitation. He was extra strong against sexual abuse situations, particularly rape and pedophilia. He was strong for the "Three strikes and you're out!" police policies, where violence was a part of it. He was dead-set against pornography. Period. Not in his community.

Trying to atone? It still didn't quite connect. This kind of stuff wasn't handled anywhere near the place. It wasn't at all likely that he was seen and recorded with some known drug dealers or such. That could be explained away with the, "I didn't have any *idea*!" line. He was at a party, they were there, he spoke to other people at parties. He didn't invite anyone like that to his parties. They came with someone else.

It was going to take a lot of digging, that was sure. There was something other than laundering that was behind it. Maybe they had recordings of him using drugs?

No. He wouldn't be at any parties with that bunch on Bastimentos. They moved in entirely different circles. It was strange that they ever were in the same place at the same time for them to have made any recordings.

Maybe a brothel? He was so adamant about sexual matters. Maybe they would meet him by chance in a whorehouse, somewhere. That would mean Bianco or Herman having a connection. The men, it was obvious why they would see him. They might well be clients of such places, but the women would be connected only as madams or working girls. That was a line to investigate. Look at it from the other side.

He worked on Julia Bianco. She seemed to be a girl from a small town in Alabama, had left the state to go to college in Houston, Texas, had never finished for a degree, dropping out in her third semester when her grades made it plain she wasn't going to get any degree there. She went to Southern California, to a small college, where she finished her degree in Agriculture. She was a registered veterinarian there for two years before moving to LA. Little was known of her since. She communicated with people she knew from college and back home with letters or phone calls until three years ago, when she started using the net and Skype. She had a blog for awhile. It was actually dull. She didn't say much and communicated with people she met at her trade. She mentioned pets, now and then on it, giving advice on cures and training. She liked rodeo and stock car racing and was into country music, trying to play the piano, but hadn't gotten anywhere with it. She admitted she couldn't sing. She wasn't very good as a pianist. She hung around a place near where she lived for awhile in Santa Clara, called the Streetcorner Bar. She dated a man, once in awhile, and seemed to keep her relationships to one at the time for a minimum of several months.

Unless she was damned good at fantasy writing, she never worked a brothel, or even the streets or bar stools.

Frieda Herman was born near Bakersfield, California. She was raised on a small farm. She had been married to a man who she caught in another man's bed. He was bi, and she loved him, but she wouldn't take the chances that brought to a relationship, what with AIDS being so bad, especially in California. They used the computer to stay in touch, about once a month. She didn't use it much more than that. There wasn't much about her to be found. She had stayed in a rented apartment in the poorer section of San Mateo for two years before coming to Panamá.

Okay. The brothel idea wasn't behind it.

He looked up Lucerne while he was at it. Not much. Raised in Baton Rouge, Louisiana, went to LSU for two years, finished at UCLA. Had a bit of trouble when he slept with a sixteen year old girl, but she admitted she had convinced him she was nineteen, in court. The state dropped the charges her parents had brought against her when she had claimed that her father had molested her when she was thirteen until she was almost fifteen. She wouldn't testify that he had direct relations with her, only that he was always feeling her up. He was a party animal, to an extent, but didn't care for the regular upper class parties. He liked the more countrified places and stayed in a semi-barrio town called Carnivalitas.

Sick bastard!

That left Clint about where he was when he started. It wasn't from recording a drug use or in a brothel.

Clint went back to Napoli and studied a picture. He was a semi-handsome man. He probably had very little trouble getting dates.

Police records were his main hope. He could use the connection with the Policia Nacional to get information about him.

There was nothing in Carmel or the immediate area, except parking tickets and a careless driving ticket, six years ago. He was carrying a young boy somewhere and swerved off the road when the kid spilled grape juice all over his Mercede's hand-tooled leather seat. 1997.

Maybe the record was elsewhere. Santa Clara?

He had two parking tickets there, a year and a month apart. By a fireplug once and another yellow curb violation at the central park.

Carnivalitas? He had to go to Mapquest to even find out where it was. It was three-quarters Mexicans. Lucerne spoke fair Spanish. He could communicate fairly well. Napoli had lodged a complaint there because two of his hubcaps had been stolen.

So. He had been to all those places for some reason.

What about Danny Lesterinni?

A hour and a half and Clint knew that he was born in Denver, Colorado, but had moved to Phoenix, Arizona, when his father's job moved there. He was about four years old. At nine, he was living in Oregon, then Washington state, then down to San Francisco, until he went to LA a month before he moved to Panamá.

Napoli had a string of parking tickets in several parts of the San Francisco area. It seemed he would park his fancy car somewhere and not get back before the meter expired or such. There was a definite connection with something. Napoli was going to the poorer sections of a lot of places for some reason.

Clint checked with Mapquest on the exact locations the tickets were issued. Near parks, movie theaters, bus stations – that rang a bell! Was Napoli gay?

Not that he could find, but this guy was trying hard for whatever it was not to be known. In California, who would make a stink if he was? They were far too liberal about that too ever make it a problem. Unless...?

Unless there was more to it than that. He didn't have AIDS. He was far too public a person to hide it in his own community.

Okay. Into pornography, which was why he was so adamant about it coming into his own community? He was the type, to look at, who would appear in those things.

No. Those things were made for money. He didn't need money.

That left ... what?

So!

"Manny, I think I know what they have on him, but there's no way I can check that I know about. I know your family was never into porno, but this isn't really that. You had women. Did you have gay contacts?"

"If there was a market for it, we had a thumb or two in. Porno works, if you have the right women – or men, for the gay trade. Anything we did there was because they came to us for financing. We never trapped anybody into that kind of thing. You knew Pops. You can't begin to picture him into ... Christ! He's into young girls or boys?"

"I don't know. It's all I'm left with."

"That wouldn't make much of a splash in California. He could buy out of that. It would do it to his reputation, though. There are male and female hustlers there that are barely old enough to get it up. We refused to use anyone underage."

"I found where he had a traffic ticket in 1997 with an eleven year old boy in the car. It's not his kid, there's nothing I can find that would make him an uncle or such. Why the kid was there wasn't mentioned."

There was a silence. "Pedophile?"

"I just don't know! I sure as all the levels of hell don't want to start any rumors or accusations because I can't find anything else likely. He could be some kind of spy, or something."

"I'll try to get some kind of information on it. There are people in almost any town in California who we can use. Gimme names and dates and so forth. If there's anything there, we'll find it."

Clint gave him the list. He then went back to the

computer to try other searches. Almost any kind of porno was on the net. Very little kiddie porn. He didn't want that kind of site on his hard drive.

An hour for nothing. He went to town for a good meal at the Rip Tide, then met Dave, Judi, Earl, and Ben. They went around town to all the places they usually visited. It was a good night, particularly when Marianne, a girl he'd met a year before, when she was there on vacation, called him and asked if he was busy tonight. She was back for three days, then was headed for San Blas. He said he'd meet her at Toro Loco.

"Clint? Sergio here," greeted him about ten o'clock in the morning. "It looks like another of our lovely Bastimentos residents has found her way to the morgue. Julia Bianco."

"Same MO?"

"Yes and no. Different cause of death, torture employed. Some of it was while she was still alive. She was hit over the head with something. I'd say a piece of that rerod that's laying around. The first blow only stunned her, then she was worked over a little, killed, and beaten some more. I'd say an amateur who didn't know if it was enough, so kept on. Messy."

"She hadn't been anywhere else but the finca?"

"She went into Bocas Town late yesterday afternoon for groceries. She went to the internet café next door to the big China. She went to the wine shop. She had dinner at Nine Degrees. She went back. She wasn't any worse than usual, but she wasn't any better, either."

"Franconi in town?"

"I don't think so. I'm having my men check him out."

"What the hell is with those people? There's no way ... I'll be damned!"

“What?”

“I have to check on some things. I’ll call you back.”

Clint called Manny and asked if there was a way that Napoli would know they were checking into his past. It was possible they asked someone some questions who had former contact with him. That was always a risk in the business.

He called Sergio back and said he wanted to go out there to talk to them. Sergio said he was there. Come on out.

He got in his boat and made a quick trip to the island. He tied up at the dock and went to the house to find the bunch of them sitting around the great room.

“I think something I’ve done resulted in Bianco getting murdered,” he announced. “Whichever one of you is the plant, nobody here had anything to do with my investigation into his past. It was something that happens a lot in international cases. You check out everyone’s past. I can tell each of you a lot about yourself. Knocking off Bianco was immensely stupid. My investigation was coming up empty, but this tells me I’m dead on target. If you got orders from Napoli for this, you can tell him it gave me a direction. I’ll find it now. I never give up.”

“What the hell?! You meddle around in his affairs and get us all killed, and it’s just so sad?!” Catherine cried. “Oh, my god! If it’s coming out anyhow, we’re all as good as dead!”

“Part of the blackmail business. You places your bet and takes your chances,” Clint replied. “Lesterinni and Bianco didn’t hedge their bets enough. I don’t give a hoot in hell about any of you. Just no more killing. It’s too late to hide it, now.”

They mumbled at each other. They didn’t have a clue

as to which one was the plant. Clint had one very strong possibility in mind.

"I want to know where each one of you was, and with whom, since early last night until the body was discovered this morning."

"Well, I was with Henry all night! He's my *husband*, after all!" Catherine said.

"We were together all afternoon and all last night," Dickerson said.

Doc came in and said she was dead for six to seven hours. He could get it much closer at the morgue. Clint thanked him.

"It's now ten forty five. She was killed around three o'clock," Clint said. "That's the time you have to tell me about."

"Nothing to tell," Frieda Herman said. "I spent the night with Frank. We were together until about five thirty."

"Neither of you left the room, even for ten minutes?"

"Not for any minutes," Lucerne agreed. "That's a particular time I would have very damned well remembered if she wasn't there, you can bet!"

"It had to be Franconi!" Catherine wailed. "You said it wasn't him, but it *has* to be! I was *asleep* at that hour!"

"Napoli can hire fifty Franconis. He wouldn't blink," Dickerson said. "I think it must have been him or some other thug he hired. He messes with me, he'll wish he was never born!"

"If it comes out from another source, you don't have anything to bargain with anymore," Clint said. "I *will* get you!"

They looked at each other. They were mutually suspicious, now. It was a very unpleasant feeling.

Clint went out and talked with Sergio a few minutes,

then headed back home. His main suspect might have an alibi. Crap!

"Who do you think it is?" Judi asked. She'd brought over some sticky buns she made.

"Did think," Clint answered. "Lucerne. He was only around a couple of weeks before they came here."

"Oh. Right. Logical. How will you find out who it is?"

"I think I have to come from the angle of who it isn't."

"Chop off everything that doesn't look like part of an elephant, you end up with a statue of an elephant."

"Only if you get the parts in the right places." She gave him the finger.

He spent the afternoon around his house, then went into town. Franconi was getting off the water taxi when he passed, so he asked where he'd been before Sergio could get to him.

"Santa Marta, Colombia. I had a quick job there. Why?"

"Bianco got offed."

"Why? Now it doesn't make sense to me."

"Because I was investigating Napoli, I suppose. Someone added two and two and got thirteen point five."

"You're investigating him?"

"Certainly! They're blackmailing him to the tune of six million dollars."

"Could be, but I think I'd know about anyone else here. Anyone in the trade. Professional job?"

"No. Messy. Any idea which one's the plant?"

"Would he do that? I guess so. I haven't paid that much attention. I just watch them."

"Dickerson says he could hire fifty like you. He could be right."

"As amateur as it is, he might have hired the wrong one. I doubt it was from him, but it could be. I don't think he ever met them before the meeting that brought them here. Not to notice, anyhow."

"He has to notice. It's his only security. He's in this because he tends to not notice things that can be traced."

"Such as?"

"Parking tickets."

"Ah! And you started wondering why he was where he got those tickets?"

"More or less."

"I think maybe I'd better get paid pretty fast or I might not get paid at all."

"Is he fool enough to try to stiff his hit man?"

Franconi laughed. Clint waved and went on.

Now he was going to have to decide where his next step laid. He wasn't going to get anything from that bunch on Bastimentos. He would try to get something through Manny, but that was more and more doubtful. Napoli knew he was under close investigation. He was covering. That he knew meant some pretty powerful connections in California. Manny not knowing about him at all showed he had one hell of an organization.

He was going to have to go to California. Crap!

He had a good disguise or two. He could pull it off. The only problem was getting to California without Napoli knowing.

He got an idea. He went to call on Judi. It might work, if he timed it right. There were places he went when he wanted to relax or think for a day or two. He hoped he wouldn't have to be in the states more than that.

Judi said she'd go along with it. She could tell them he was close by letting things slip. She was an expert at that, and at getting information from the locals they didn't know they gave her.

He took the bus to the comarca. Clint Faraday got off

the bus. An hour later Peter Bushnell, who had a slight resemblance to him, but who walked and talked different, caught a bus to Panamá City. He got off in Santiago and caught a hopper plane to San Jose', Costa Rica, where his flight was booked to LA as of two weeks ago.

Manny could arrange that kind of thing.

Clint got off the company plane at the private field and took a taxi to the Royal Palm Hotel. He was a bit stooped and had a barely noticeable hitch when he walked. He kept poking his glasses up on his nose. The expensive wig was just off-color enough that it was noticeable, but was of excellent quality. That hid the fact he had a thick mop of his own hair. People would picture him as balding. His eyes were an odd green color. He tended to look at his expensive wristwatch every two or three minutes.

He booked in, then went to his room to rest from the trip. He would go to a little place near Carmel, later, to give a report on some medicinal plants found in Panamá (true facts. Dave was a botanist who studied that kind of thing. He had given him a report to give to some friends in Carmel) to try to get financing to research the truth about them. His reports were necessarily mostly anecdotal, though there were lists of some of the compounds found in the plants. People interested in promoting natural medicines and cures were invited from all the nearby areas. This was the kind of thing Napoli wouldn't miss.

Clint arrived at the community center half an hour before he was due to speak. He mingled with the people and learned a few things that might help him with this project. If he got a grant, Dave would use it to augment his teaching of students from Universidad de Panamá.

Napoli came in with a bit of an entourage to sit near front and center. Clint recognized him immediately from the photos on the net. He seemed to be an affable type. He was definitely popular.

Clint spent two hours plus on the presentation, mostly answering questions. He kept telling them that a friend did the actual work. He just kept the records and took pictures (which he brought along on a CD to show). Dave taught him all he knew about the plants.

After the meeting Napoli said he should come by his office in the suburbs tomorrow to discuss the grant. It was important and useful work. This was the kind of thing that those people with the resources should finance for the good of all. He had friends in Panamá. He had heard there were several groups in the country who were doing such research. If this Dave character he kept referring to was doing this at his own expense, and was *not* financed by some drug company that would curtail research if some cheap and easily available cure were to be found for a problem, he would fund him, all the way. That would be the agreement, no sales or gift of his research to a greedy commercial enterprise. If a patent could be attained for any process he developed it would be in the name of Napoli Diversified. It would be free to the world.

He got instructions to Fallendale Heights and went back to the hotel room. He couldn't agree with Napoli on that part more. Clint couldn't picture him in any sordid or perverted situation.

The office was impressive and understated. It was impressive *because* it was understated. As Clint went into the receptionist's stand, Napoli was coming out of a hallway toward the rear. He was with a slightly younger man who resembled him. He waved to Clint and spoke intensely to the younger man as Clint approached. The man started walking away as Clint got to them. Napoli said, "My brother, Gino. Peter Bushnell." Clint got a dead fish handshake, and Gino walked away.

"Come on into my office, Peter. I only have about five minutes of work to do, then we can discuss your friend's project. There's coffee and donuts on the desk. Help yourself."

Clint went into the plush inner office, which was comfortable-bordering-on-penthouse-suite. He grabbed a pecan Danish and poured a large mug of gourmet coffee. Napoil returned five minutes later and sat in an armchair next to Clint. He said the desk was for business. This was more a chat about personal projects, so would be informal.

"I checked on your friend in Panamá. He is a local character who was once a mid-profile musician and writer. He's still a writer of fiction and research into orchids, has been all over the world. He is overly-loud and stubborn about the natives.

"I mean the Indios, not the imports.

"He is friends with a Taiwanese woman, a gay man, a detective, locals, and the Indios. He is considered a bit of a nutcase by many.

"He also does the research you spoke of. He does fund as many poor students as his very limited funds will allow in the universities, on the condition they remain in the top percentile of their classes. All of them have done so, one becoming top student in the university in the chosen field.

"Many think he is gay. He does not deny nor confirm it, saying always that it is no one's business who is gay or who isn't, so long as he is not involved, personally. He only goes so far as to state perhaps he is bi to one extent or another.

"I am interested in that only so far as it would affect his work, and only so far as it does *not, in any way, ever*, affect children. I have known a pedophile, and am adamantly opposed to placing such people in any situation that would involve or in any way encourage their activities.

"Is he gay, which does not matter, and is there any least hint of pedophilia?"

"He is probably bi. He has ladyfriends, as he calls them, in several places. He also is close friends with some gay people. He has a son and grandkids in another Central American country. When it comes to pedophilia, he believes, and states very clearly, that those people should get a bullet between the eyes. It's the only way they'll stop.

"He also often states a child is different ages in different places. In Panamá, most thirteen year old kids know more about sex that I do. In the states, here, they are children until they're in their late teens, in some cases. He thinks, as I do, that it's a matter where the knowledge and experience makes the adult.

"There's no way an undeveloped prepubescent child is not a child. In Panamá, as a place where he knows the details of life, he says he considers them children until about thirteen, though some places, the age of consent, the local feelings, is twelve. That's much too young for his or my acceptance. They just think they know what it's all about. They know shit!

"He wouldn't consider anything with a girl under the legal age, seventeen, and he doesn't date anyone nearly that young. He dated one who was twenty three in Bocas, but not often. He likes a woman in her late twenties or early thirties.

"Is this about your brother?"

"What makes you think that?"

"Because I shook his hand out there. It was a rather

unpleasant experience."

He studied Clint a moment, sighed, and said he at least had fears about such things with Gino.

"Peter, why haven't anyone but a Judi Lum, a Manny Mathews, a Ben Longstreet, and Dave ever heard of you?"

"I met with them when I was with Dave in David and, once, in Almirante. I worked with Dave in the field where I was staying in San Felix with the Indios. They are *my* favorite people, too. I wasn't around the people he associates with, except when we were in town for supplies. Memory sticks and a new camera, in my case. I used the internet in Almirante when I went through, one time, and met Ben. He's gay, a friend of Dave's, and the others.

"Dave and I talked a lot in the field. We met so many different people among the Indios. They're a very diverse group."

He nodded and sat back to sip coffee and think.

"You state he is honest in his dealings with everyone, to the extent he alienates some of them. In what way?"

"He deliberately challenges those people who are spouting that bullshit, particularly about other people. Always, when it's about the Indios. He faces down bigots, though he admits that a certain situation made a bigot of him, in a limited way. He despises snobs with attitude. That kind of thing. He says he answers to one person in the universe. He has to meet the eyes of that person, directly, when he shaves in the morning. If he can't meet those eyes, he's a piece of shit.

"I agree. I use the definition, myself."

He sat back to think again. "I'll give you a check for a hundred thousand dollars, right now, then more, as needed, determined by Dave. If what I've heard is true, that will finance him for years."

"No. It'll finance things for a couple of months, but Dave'll have another dozen students in the universities with everything he doesn't need – and he needs next to nothing, for himself – in days."

He laughed. "That, I'll finance! *If* he holds to the rules as you've stated them. He, apparently, chooses those to help well."

"That, he does. He's a bit stupid about personal things. He trusts all the wrong people, then he digs in and becomes hardnosed with the ones he considers worth his time. It's how he is."

"It is true that he owns a hotel and several parcels of land that are in another's name? That it was stolen from him because he trusted a charismatic scam artist?"

"Yes. He's never going to let that go, for which I don't blame him. He'll see those crooks in jail or dead. He says that they prey on retirees, who can't afford it."

They chatted for a few minutes, then Clint said he had to go. He would probably be in town for another day, then back to the field. Napoli asked if he needed anything. He said he got by and was comfortable enough. He didn't need much.

Clint felt as though he had met a truly good person. Manny had been wrong about him. That didn't mean he made all that money through legitimate channels. He probably did that just like Manny suggested, but it wasn't him who got into the crooked parts, and it wasn't him who was doing that bit in Panamá and Bastimentos. Clint wanted a way to get rid of Napoli's albatross without it affecting him personally.

Clint got off the plane, went to the hotel in Santiago, cleaned up, and became Clint Faraday again, then went to have a good dinner in the place across the street. He missed the local fare in only two days!

He decided to spend the night in Santiago, so went to the popular local bar nearby to swap stories about anything that came up. It was a very pleasant night. He was up early for the bus to David, stayed there a day, then went to Bocas. He hadn't let anyone know he was back, yet, so went to Judi's place, to find she was with some friends who wanted to see Panamá. She was at Las Tablas and places farther out the peninsula. She was coming back via Chitre the day after tomorrow.

He saw Dave and told about the conversation and handed him the check. He was surprised, and told Clint he was elected to make all the speeches he was supposed to make and wouldn't. He would put another couple dozen people through university with the money! He would also accept as much as Napoli wanted to send.

He agreed with Clint about getting Gino out of the picture.

"Your super good friends – to hear them tell it – on Bastimentos – are worried that they might not be allowed to leave. Ever."

"I think I can make them ... I think maybe one of them, at least, can be made to turn on the boss! That may be a solution! I'll let them all know the killer's head's in the noose. I can drop the trap the minute I get confirmation from him. The boss is Gino. I'll have to arrange for them to get out of Panamá, but I want to know who, first. I want the others tagged and watched. I don't like blackmailers, regardless of who or why they do it."

"You use blackmail yourself, so don't get holy on me," Dave said, grinning.

"I use *threatened* blackmail on them."

"There's a difference?"

Clint gave him the bird.

He called Manny to tell him the story. He accepted that it could well be true, that Napoli was Italian – and they were his people. He knew what he would put up with and would always try to protect his family from getting caught, in most things.

"Clint, that's duty. If someone else gets them, that's the way of life. If they had reason, you say it was fated to happen and move on. If they don't have reason they get stepped on."

"There's reason to go around with this one, I'd say. I want to find who's the killer in the bunch. I'll probably arrange for them to go home just before I get the information for a deal with the FBI with him to take his brother down to protect certain people. He'll have to squeal on whoever's his hit here to get the deal."

"Oh. He'll put all his crooked shit on Napoli. That happens among the type. He would know they can put him away for life for his pedophilia, so will make any deal he can.

"Napoli wouldn't turn on his brother for any reason. Gino will turn on him or anyone else in a flash. They all know it."

"So they have to prevent that. Gino was blackmailing them, so they have reason."

"You can make it work."

They talked about any new information. There was damned little of it.

Clint went into town to talk with Sergio, then found

Franconi, and chatted with him. He said his boss was about to go down hard, so get whatever's owed, right away. Franconi thanked him and laughed.

"I don't know what it's about, but my boss, who you found out is not Napoli, is a pervert, if I ever saw one. He got caught with the wrong person in a perverted situation, as they say?"

"Uh-huh. That bunch out there found him in the wrong place at the wrong time with the wrong person. People, considering all of them."

"Now I have to wonder if he'll turn on me."

"A risk of the business."

He nodded. They talked for a few more minutes, then Clint went home, got his boat, and headed for Bastimentos. He was just in time to find Catherine and Lucerne in one of the gazebos. They were below eye level, where he didn't see them until he was passing four feet away. They didn't see him.

He started thinking. Some things suddenly began to click. At the house, Dickerson was watching wrestling on the TV. He said he didn't know where any of the others were. This time of day, his wife was locked in her bedroom for her beauty nap, Lucerne went out fishing, probably Frieda was with him.

"I mainly dropped in to tell you to stop telling people we're friends. You're just someone I'm investigating – and to tell you your meal ticket's about to expire. Gino's ass is in a crack. The only way to save it will probably be to claim the bunch of you were blackmailing him, and that he paid one of you to start knocking off the others. You should all check your proof, because Danny lost his and died, then Julia let the wrong person know how to find her proof, and she died.

"Gino's gonna tell us who to save his own hide. It will

take a week or so to wear him down, then at least one of you goes down the hard way.

"We don't want you here. I'll try to arrange for you to get out in a way that lets the police off the hook for letting you escape. It'll have to be damned fast, so let me know within the hour if you're willing to take the chance."

He said he'd take any chance he could find to get out of Panamá. He didn't doubt that Gino would crack. He was a total wimp!

Clint went back home. It was now up to them. Dickerson would call him as soon as they were ready to leave. If anyone wanted to stay, he didn't have any say in that. He and Catherine would get out as fast as they could!

The phone buzzed half an hour after Clint got home. Dickerson said they were all ready to leave. It wouldn't take them ten minutes to get stuff because they kept it packed since the first time they wanted to get out.

"Go load the stuff on your boat. I'll have the cop there instructed to let you go, because you're going to Bocas. The police boat'll watch your every move. The police boat's gonna get an emergency call to help locate a drug runner. It will go toward Zapatillias. Go north to Costa Rica, pay someone fifty bucks to stamp your passports, then go back to the states or wherever. You shouldn't have any trouble disappearing for a month or so, there. It'll be over by then. Nobody's going to try to get a child molester's blackmailer's too hard. They'll say he deserved it and worse and be glad he's caught and is going to be put away for life.

"He'll throw you to the dogs, in a blink. They won't act on that. It's the only way to make a deal for fifteen to twenty instead of life without. He'll try to throw his brother to them, too. The one part of this deal you have to make with me is that you'll tell the truth. Napoli had nothing to do with it."

They agreed to that in a flash. Clint said to wait five minutes, then get to the dock and get on that boat as fast as they can. He'll give them a call the second the police boat's been dispatched to the Zapatillas.

"One of you is going to have to be able to disappear completely. He's going to have to give whichever one of you who's acting as a hired killer here up. That's the only deal they'll make to give him anything to hang onto.

"That's fine with me! They're going to start the hard pressure right away and figure he'll crack in a week or less. I want you out of here. You fend for yourself after you're in international waters."

He waited four minutes then told them to go. It would take the police boat six minutes to get to the Zapatillas and six to get back when they found the drug runner had been caught just as they arrived. That made twelve minutes for them to get out of sight toward the north. They should have enough of a head start to be in Costa Rican waters before the police boat could intercept them. Then they were on their own.

He waited. Sergio called to say he didn't believe that bunch could move so damned fast. They were running like their asses were on fire. Clint said he would come to town later to get the reports on where they went. Their boat had a transponder on it that gave the GPS readings on it every ten minutes.

They went to northern Costa Rica, stayed less than an hour, then went on to Yucatan, then to Galveston. Manny had them watched. Dickerson went directly to Ohio, Lucerne went to Louisiana, Herman went to Colorado. Catherine went to LA. Just what Clint thought she'd do.

"See, everybody else had air-tights for Bianco's murder. Hers was Dickerson, his was her. He sleeps like a log, as they say where he came from. He drinks six or eight beers, then sacks out. He's really out!

"She's screwing anybody with the time and energy, I'd say. She's very used to sneaking away at night, but she was doing it during the day, too. She was locked in her room for her beauty nap, so far as Dickerson knew, but was in that gazebo with Lucerne. You can bet it was a long number from the first time."

"That one, you pegged," Manny agreed. "She's a type. You find three of her in every redneck bar in the world! Anyhow, let's see what transpires."

They talked for a few more minutes, then Clint decided he could use a beauty nap. Trouble was, he couldn't sleep during the day, anytime.

So he went fishing.

"Hi! I'm home!" Judi greeted. "Did you learn anything new in California?"

"I learned that Arno Napoli had nothing to do with what's here past the financing of the moving of those scum on Bastimentos. I didn't figure who killed them until I was back."

"It was that Frank character, right?"

"No. Catherine."

"Really?"

"Dead certain."

"You let them go? Sergio said you and he made a plan to get them out of here. Panamá doesn't need the headaches and expense of prosecuting them."

"Uh-huh. It's better to have them back in the states with their redneck friends than here in jail."

"I'm beginning to see your point about that with some of these ... people who come here."

"It's about being pragmatic."

"I guess. Want to come to the Nine Degrees for dinner? I don't want to cook tonight. I'm tired.

"Oh! Serg said to tell you Franconi left within minutes of that bunch sailing into the sun ... rise. We're east."

"I figured he would. Let's go get some of Rick's cooking!"

"... saw that he was the brother of the very esteemed personage in Fallendale, Mr. Arno Napoli. The police report it appeared to be an attempted robbery that went wrong. He was stabbed seven times.

"Services will be held at the Fallendale Mother of Mercy Hospital chapel tomorrow. It is to be a closed, private ceremony, as Mr. Arno Napoli states that the circumstances and the wishes of the family are for such arrangements. In other news, there were two more drive-by...."

Clint turned off the cable TV tuned to LA CBS, shook his head, and wondered. Did Franconi get him and make it look like the MO of Catherine? Did Catherine get him? Did Manny have it done?

He might never know the real story. He wasn't sure he wanted to. Now, today. Fishing?

No. Maybe to Tierra Oscura, where Dave was doing his research. He liked that.

Or ....

C. D. Moulton's works are available on most major outlets as printed or e-books. CD writes the CD Grimes, PI, mysteries, the Det. Lt. Nick Storie mysteries, the Clint Faraday mysteries, the Flight of the Maita science fiction series, books on orchid culture and many others of many types. Mystery, adventure, intrigue, science fiction, humor, fantasy, paranormal, mild erotica, and factual.